Accident Prone

TwentyTwoTwos Vol. 2

By: Rocky Mullin

Self Published
Self Created
Self Edited
Self Crafted
For Himself
By Himself

Praise to Yeshua, Glory be to God.

This book is dedicated to my Papa.
May his soul rest as mine does the heavy lifting now.

This year has brought many things.

Temptation

Closure

Greif

And Reflection.

Upon these things I have realized that my passion is driven by the situations around me.

Like an actor diving deep into a part, I dive deep into the words I put to paper. I try to live by the words I write and open my mind, soul and body to creating something that represents me. Whether you like me, love me, hate me, or dont know me, I am here.

I've decided to turn your thoughts on your head.

Flipping the painting upside down and forcing you

to look at it.

Drowning you with thoughts you don't fully

understand yet.

Allowing you a glimpse into my brain that makes

you question your own.

the creative genius that is rocky Mullin

I pray I become successful enough that people come to me for advice like I wish I could have with someone.

A Memoir.

I can't sing, dance, or play a song. I can't run fast or lift heavy things anymore. I have become normal, and that is sickening to me. The idea that Rocky can't be a persona. He can't live a double life that masks the deep ideas in his mind. So, I had to confront myself. I had to take a LONG hard look in the mirror, decide who I wanted to be. With those brown eyes staring right back at me I made my decision. I would use my peculiar intellect, and I would create a voice. If you've spoken to me, you know the emotion and brass that my voice carries. Filled with emotion, tone and deep meaning I speak my truths. My hidden power inside me has created a new version of myself. One that when I relook in the mirror, I see someone with power within their words, someone who can place any idea into a sentence and make it make sense. A man with a goal. A goal to change his life, to reinvent himself again and again. Take the bad and get rid of as much of it as you can. Remove the doubt within the fear of rejection or humiliation. Allow myself to fully engulf the new age that is this period of my life. Because long gone are the times of football pads and helmets, gone are the convertible BMWs, gone is the kid who couldn't use his voice. A powerful tool most can't find within themselves is the power of words. More importantly putting those words together to form a sentence worthwhile. And furthering that creating a sentence that changes the mind and view of someone else. That Rocky is dead, and I am what remains.

The values and morals of man shift daily. As the wind moves so does the heart of man. He hates this and loves that, and then loves that and hates this. To shift the mind is to change the way you think. To dive deep into the thought of something is human nature. The scholars and philosophers of our past did just this. Changing the shape of society as they knew it. They allowed their brain to conjure up ideas, giving them the full view on what the world they saw was. But it's just that, it's what they saw. We all see the color red, unless you're colorblind. We all see that money is green and that air is clear, two things essential to life. But as one person views money as nothing but a constellation prize, others view it as life or death. One person views air as something given so they shall take, but others see it as a liberty in the world we live in. To shape new ideas, you must take old ones, view them, analyze them, live them, and finally decide if you want to change them. You have to endure the suffering of those ideas to create new ones. Without suffering there is no real human experience. Without pain there is no growth. When you break a bone that bone grows back stronger, when you break your brain, it takes longer for that wound to heal. To understand the past, you have to look to the future. To see what caused that change before and what will cause that change again. With many people that change never comes. They change how they see things, but they don't change the view in front of them.

This is a representation of the thoughts inside my brain.

Part 1

Temptation

temp·ta·tion

/tem(p)ˈtāSH(ə)n/

1. The desire to do something, especially wrong or unwise
2. A thing or course of action that attracts or temps someone

LACERATION.

To resist the urges is like rejecting myself.

To urge to text you,

To say, "**Why not now**?"

Or "**This time is different**."

I stop myself time after time after typing a love story in my text box.

Urgently I wait to hear a chime that my urge has been met.

But before I do, I feel the puddle behind me begin to grow.

The blood marks the pain you've caused, and the desperation I have for you.

The ever-dying need of your attention and approval.

I cannot go on with this knife in my back, but when I pull it out you go with it.

So, I keep it lodged deep into my tissues, buried
inside my muscle fibers, to remind myself that a
little bit of you is still there, residing inside me.

PRODITO.

With a lock and a key, you stored yourself within

me.

Allowing me to infiltrate your mind and know

things no one else would.

Put your trust in me without a care.

Because I did just that, showed you I cared.

With a glimmer in my eye and swift with my words

I gave you a place you could place your heart.

And with that you sealed your fate.

Succumbing to your deadly wound given by me.

Breaking the lock and gashing you dastardly.

Betraying the trust you placed within me and

creating a hole in you that cannot be sealed.

Dying in my arms.

CLICKS AND LIKES.

I scroll every day.

Seeing post after post

Name after name.

But yours, yours sticks out.

I see it in the crowd of people on my screen.

She posts this, he likes that.

But you, my eyes only go to you.

The alphabetical makeup of you pulls me closer.

My eyes are glued to my screen seeing you day by day.

I hope you see me like I see you.

Falling for you from less than a foot apart.

My eyes meet yours but while mine blink, yours light up in LED.

HEROIN.

I want to inject you into my veins and watch the blood run down my arm.

Allow you to take control of my life and hold me hostage.

Take my goals and values and make me steal.

Steal every second from you, every embrace, every fiber of your being.

I crave you so bad it gives me headaches.

Drives me up the walls, I'm leaving scratch marks on the door, the door to you.

The door I so badly want to be opened.

But it's locked from the outside and all I can do is grasp.

I stare at your feet from underneath hoping to hear the door click and my high return.

NARCISSISMUS.

A savior who leads me to grace.

Allows me to engulf myself in the work of my past and future.

Giving me the tools to form the ideas forthcoming.

With this I take my sword and cut open all that is in front of me.

The lust and greed power me through as I strike down my enemies with precision.

Living a life that only those of hate and anger would envy.

Taking things for myself, pillaging the lands and stealing from the poor.

Lining my pockets with tears and pain.

Taking my loot to the bank of things money can't buy.

I thank the savior by looking in the mirror and

giving a wink.

Glancing at him in the windows as I pass by.

Admiring the work he has done by looking into my

own hands.

LUCIOUS.

I stalk my prey and trap them with bait.
Laying out my intentions with hidden premonition.
Luring them in with the appeal of love and attentiveness.
Knowing that a deceitful and indolent path lies ahead.
With a smile on my face, I hold the knife behind my back, and when they embrace, I strike.
I wait until they are vulnerable so that the kill is easy.
My work is done when I feel their body drop limp and their soul disperse.
I lay them down with an ear-to-ear grin knowing that another name can be added to the list.
I hide them away for no one to find, but they still live in the back of my mind.

TIGHTS IN NIGHTTIME, DAYTIME EVERYONE RUNS.

I line my soldiers up accordingly.
Place your left foot there and your right one better be where I say.
I usually make them do rigorous tasks to weed out the weak ones.
I don't think they know I pick favorites though.
I let them jog slower, so they still look pretty when the run is over.
So that their hair isn't all greasy and full of knots, it's easier to run my fingers through.
Many show up to my camp but most of them fail.
The bigger ones are always the first to go, I make them run in the front and by the end they're in the back, even with the pretty ones jogging.

The middle of the pack is usually around for a few weeks, until they get tired of how I treat the prettier ones.

And eventually even the pretty ones leave, with growing jealousy inside them they refuse to compete with someone else.

In the end they all usually go, until there are none left, and the next batch gets ready to step up to the challenge.

THE ADULTRESS.

You take me in with open arms as I fall deeply into
your lust.
Your breasts against me allude evil thoughts.
As we lean to your bed, my soul begins to separate
from my body and enter the depths of hell.
Your soft hand against my face as you tell me
everything's okay allows me to engulf all that I am
into you.
Praying that we morph into one and that I never
have to leave you.
Putting a tumor inside your brain so that you never
forget me.
Every time that you bring me in it makes me never
want to leave.
You slow time down to distract me from the fact
that eternal damnation is coming.

Your words taste like honey and your touch is like

silk.

You fulfill the prophecy of the adulteress in my life.

I LIED.

I told myself I wouldn't write about you.

I told you I wouldn't write about you.

But I can't help it.

Without you I cease to be who I am.

While you shaped me so much when you were here,

it was after the fact that did the most.

Because without you I learned far more than I did

with you.

A speck of dust is what you showed me, the entire

universe is what I received when we said our

goodbyes.

The knowledge of myself and others around me.

Knowing that not everyone cares for you the way

you do them.

That sometimes in life you must do things alone.

And others you'll be forced to be alone.

You can hope and pray all you want but a well is only good when it is drinkable.

BALL ROOM.

I look in the shadows and don't find you lurking.
I hope to see you behind me as I eagerly wait for your return.
As I think you're searching for me, I stay searching for you; and I think that's where we miss each other.
I continue my search hoping that you will be shown in the light.
The shadows I search are dark and cold.
They speak to me, telling me that you aren't there.
They say you've never been there.
I dismiss their claims and continue to search, allowing myself to dive deeper and deeper into these places no man should enter.
I become one with the shadow and lose my body, but my soul remains.

I walk through the world now without form, sliding
in and out, having an absence of self.
I continue my search into the light, but it's too late
for me.
I no longer do this to find you, but to find myself.
But, when I finally find you.
Your light shines so bright, your essence slowly
brings mine back.
I see you spinning around dancing with bliss.
I get so close to you, but you can't see me.
My hands begin to form as I reach out and begin to
grab your arm.
But the shadows rip me back, pulling me away from
my ultimate goal.
They shred me to pieces and force me back to where
I belong.

The touch just felt like the wind to you, but to me, it

was everything.

| Sacrifice

Genius

Gen·ius:

/ˈjēnyəs/

1. Exceptional intellect or creative power or other natural ability
2. A person who is exceptionally intelligent or creative, either generally or in some particular respect
3. **Rocky Mullin**

Part 2

Closure

clo·sure

/ˈklōZHər/

1. An act or process of closing something, especially an institution, thoroughfare, or of being closed
2. (In a legislative Assembly) a procedure for ending a debate or vote

THE REAL PERSON IS THE ONE ON THE SIDE OF THE MIRROR.

I have been loved and I have been hated.
But I don't think anyone could hate nor love me more than I do myself.
The person I see in the mirror spites me every day.
He calls me fat, says my face is bent, that my teeth aren't straight.
But he's the same one who tells me I'm a genius, that I am brave and courageous, that I am such a good person.
He often switches stances to whatever seems to be happening.
He beats me like I have never been beat before.
He slashes at me for every subtle failure in his eyes.
He hugs me for doing something no one else would consider good but him.

He nearly killed me a couple of times,

but I don't think that he could ever really hurt me.

Nothing that would be fatal, he loves me just too much.

But there are times I wonder why he does the things he does.

Why does he walk with such confidence but lacks so much?

How he holds his head high despite putting it in places so low.

When he speaks to others, he sounds so full of life

but on the inside, he is completely dead.

MIDNIGHT.

I will never be the man you need me to be because

that man doesn't exist, and he never will.

You've developed this idea from Disney stories and

fairytales.

Your childhood dreams you envisioned would come

true, but your 20s have shown you different.

While I paraded around and waited for your arrival

you never came. I realized I wasn't your prince long

before you did, but I wanted to be so badly.

I poked and prodded, drove myself to insanity to be

perfect for you.

My eyes become bloodshot from the stress of being

the man you so desired.

Eventually, I gave up.

You just didn't let me.

THE ETERNAL WISH OF FAME.

A sacred beast is not to be touched.

The life of it is special and to be honored.

It is a beacon of light for those around it.

With the masses basking in its glory.

With time passing the beast continues to be praised.

I sit in the shadows and plot away.

Wanting to take the shine for me.

To mask myself so people flock to my door.

One night I steal the beast, I tie it up and lock it in a cage.

I only open it up when I arrive in a dark and secret space.

With its light illuminating all around, my knees buckle, and I fall to the ground.

When my eyesight comes to life from being blinded by the light, I see the beast crying, not sad tears, but joyful ones.

Confused, I hit the beast and told it to stop.

But the light grew so big and bright.

It looked like a star you'd see in the night.

When I came to and looked around, I couldn't see my body anymore.

My hands were gone, and my feet too.

I rushed to a mirror and burned my eyes.

I smelt the fire with my nose and my eyes had been scorched from their sockets.

The darkness I saw after that is only something one can experience for themself.

I rushed out the door and heard people clamoring, they were searching for their beast.

They grabbed me up and took me to an unknown
place.
I felt the presence of eyes all hours of the day.
Taking the place of the sacred one.
I now understand the tears of the beast.

CONDOM.

When I fell off my bike my helmet was there to protect my head.

When I slipped on the stairs the rail stopped my impact.

When I needed a loving embrace from someone, she wasn't there.

And this impact hurt far more than any other.

The stabbing pain in your chest that makes you think you're going to die.

The endless nights of tossing and turning wondering why this was the life I was given.

And no one there to comfort me.

The protection of a loving mother was withheld in my life.

When I needed the guidance to be a man, my father decided I didn't need his protection.

Protection from the world around me. The one that sets unrealistic expectations.

He just chose to shoot up and ignore the ones that were placed on him, like being a father.

His protection came in the form of a rock that when lit to 414° would mask all the responsibilities placed on him.

Ones he signed up for, and ones he didn't.

Like providing for a family, or going to work, or being a present stable father.

And when I really needed these things, I didn't get them.

When my heart got broken my mom wouldn't bat an eye.

When I needed to learn what men do, my dad was nowhere to be found.

This led to many tragedies.

Like attachment issues.

I latched on to bad people who showed me nice colors, but when those colors turned dark, I wasn't sure how to wash them away.

I know my life would be so different with protection.

I just wish my parents would have used it.

SEABIRD.

Like a seabird I sent
you to sea.
To fly your wings far and wide.
To see whales and sharks, glaciers and storms.
The setting sun and watch it rise
again.
I sit on the pier eagerly awaiting your
return.
I see ship after ship pass covered with sea birds, but
you aren't a passenger.
I wait anxiously for you, for so long.
Finally, I had enough, I decided to set sail myself to
find you.
And when I got out there, I realized why you never
came back.

NOSTALGIA IS A DRUG.

I think about you almost every day.

Most days.

When I don't it's when I flood my brain with things

that aren't you.

But sometimes you creep back in.

Then my mind begins to run a marathon of plans

about you.

I tell myself it makes so much sense, it all adds up,

the perfect equation.

I tell myself that I love your hair and your laugh

and your eyes and your smile and your

competitiveness.

I run the idea of "us" again and it's all I want.

I crave the idea to come to life.

I envy my past self for getting you.

But then the silly little thought comes back like it

does every night.

What if you don't want it, too.

Vagabond

vag·a·bond
/ˈvagəˌbänd/

1. A person who wanders from place to place without a home or job.
2. Having not a settled home.

Part 3

Grief

grief

/grēf/

1. Deep sorrow, especially caused by someone's death.
2. The feeling of sadness after losing something or someone.

My wisdom surpasses those before me, for their teachings have formed me.

THE EVERLASTING PURSUIT OF SOMETHING LIKE YOU.

I miss the way love used to be, used to be with you.
Now, they worry about if I'm financially stable or if I can pay for dates, how much my major caps out at.
Back then all you asked was if I was coming over for dinner or what random expedition we'd go on.
What parking lot we'd meet in, what we'd wear to a party.
If I could have bottled our love up, I would have sold millions.
Everyone would want a taste of what we had.
But as all things do, it spoiled and now I must sit through question after question like an interrogation.
It doesn't feel real like you did.

The weight of becoming something they want me to
be when you just let me be me.
When I realized what made me happy it was easy to
step into the life I live now.

BEETHOVEN.

I'm starting to forget the sound of your voice.

How your octaves hit my ears and caused my brain to picture you.

In a room full of voices, I used to be able to pick yours out without flaw but now, you just sound like everyone else.

Every so often I get a glimpse of you. In the smell of laundry detergent, the way a certain food tastes, or when I brush my teeth.

I forgot how your hands felt on my body or how your lips met mine.

I don't remember the smallest things and that eats alive.

I endure the pain reminiscing simply to try and keep your memory living within me.

Because forgetting you would be like forgetting a

part of myself.

SAD POEM ABOUT A GIRL

I miss the way your thumb would have to be on the outside.

Or how you would always want the right side.

How you licked your lips when you wanted a kiss.

The extended amount you would brush your teeth.

When you were mad the long look that made you look ever so beautiful.

When you were embarrassed how your face would turn a deep shade of red.

How you would look at me when we had sex.

How you would know every move I was going to make and matched it effortlessly.

How compatible we were.

How it was like a labyrinth to get to the bottom of your emotions.

How it was draining to listen to you yell at me.

How exciting it was when we wouldn't fight.

I miss that I miss fighting with you.

I miss deciphering your codes.

Understanding what made your time bomb tick.

Knowing that I held the key to your emotions.

And when we wiped all of this away it was a weight

off my shoulder.

A drink of the finest wine and drowning myself in

the cleanest of water.

Because the smell of us resided on me for years,

and you finally came back to wash it all off.

THE WAITING ROOM.

I miss the smell of the hospital.

The way the sanitizer felt on my hands.

I would put it to my nose and inhale deeply to feel

something in a place so dead.

The hard floors and ever harder seats were a

blessing compared to where you were.

The coldness of your hand felt calming in mine.

Knowing you were there was heavy on my heart but

for some reason I feel safe.

I felt safe because I knew I was with you.

NEW BALANCE.

You were so strong and providing.

So, I filled your shoes when you couldn't.

The tight hugs when someone needed them.

A bag of chips when someone was hungry.

A shoulder when someone needed to cry.

Your shoes are big, they're scarily big.

But now they are mine and I will tie them tight.

RED

I miss you. Like when it's winter and you miss the summer air. Like when the trees die, and you miss the green grass of spring. My world has become brown and dead. The day you departed a hue entered my eyesight.

I had you for 22 years.

And now I have what you've left me.

While others look at tangible things, I view the moments and lessons you brought upon me.

The teachings, the praises, the little signs of affection.

I am less of a man without you, but I am more of a man because of you. I love you more than you could ever imagine. And now that you're gone, my achievements seem less fulfilling because you will never see them.

My moments of success seem less exciting because

you will never see them.

My life goal was to make you proud.

And now I have to pray that you view them from

above and hope you smile when you see.

ROCK CHALK.

I look around and see everyone with their
respective group.
My aunts with my cousins, my cousins with their
partners, my grandma with her kids.
And then I see myself in the mirror. Alone.
The emotions hit me like a speeding truck with only
myself to lean on.
Then I turn to you, seeing you laying in a hospital
bed with cords and tubes.
You were my group; you were my safety blanket.
When I had nothing, I had you.
Seeing you die was the most painful thing I have
ever experienced.
And as I stood there alone, I realized I would now
be alone for the remainder of my life.

While everyone else had a crutch, my crutch was
fleeting to breathe.
They would still have someone to share their coffee
within the morning.
They would have someone to talk sports with.
Someone that would be proud of them.
And now, I do things with the thought of you in the
back of my mind.
Living with the memory of you, living inside of me.

R

You taught me to write my name.

I couldn't seem to figure out the “R” though.

You were patient with my little hands because you

knew how important my name would be.

You taught me to have pride in the name that was

given to me.

You showed me the old boxing movies and

reminded me my last name was Mullin.

Reminding me that a piece of you was in me.

That it was my job to build that name to more than

it was before.

Rocky Mullin.

A name with no meaning until you showed me that

everything I needed was right in my hands.

And as I wrote that broken R with confidence you
allowed me to grow in the moment, and watched
my growth through years.
Seeing that "R" slowly connect into what we see
today.

Professor X

Staring at your cold body barely hanging on was something I never expected.
For some reason I thought it would be you seeing me like that.
Your first grandson on his deathbed, my frail strength grabbing your hand instead of the other way around.
Seeing your eyes fill with tears and cheeks swollen.
You getting a headache from crying so hard.
Seeing you walk out of the room and questioning if when you come back my life will remain.
The final lesson you showed me wasn't that life sucks and you die, it was that life really sucks and you die, but you want to die with people around you. Countless hands touching yours, countless

tears falling from countless pairs of eyes, a family
holding each other with silence speaks volumes.
You always hated when we were loud, when we ran
down the hall, or knocking on your door.
So that's how we treated you in your final moments.
We walked slowly to give you time, we didn't knock
when we came in.
We sat together in silence to give your soul the
peace it needed after 65 years of struggle and
undying work.

BELOW THE DEPTHS OF THE SOUL, HIDING IN THE MIND.

I liked your eyes.

How they would pierce mine and dive deep into my soul.

You would jump off a cliff into the water below.

Reaching the bottom and finding the inner workings of me.

Kicking your feet to dive deeper, sending air bubbles above.

The lower you got the colder and darker it was.

Eventually getting so low you gasp for air, inhaling in the dark cold water that is myself.

Floating to the top with the realization that your life is fading.

Sucked from you.

Water fills your lungs until the pressure causes

them to burst.

When I pull you up and begin to try to save you,

your eyes pop out of your skull, and I get one last

look at the things that drew me so close to you.

With the realization that you are gone, I feel

nothing but remorse.

REMAIN.

In the night I sense all things.
Allowing my eyes to take a rest and my ears to open.
I hear bugs and I hear the wind.
But sometimes I faintly hear you screaming.
This does bring a smile to my face, having someone to share a moment with.
As I get closer to you, I envision the tears running down your face.
The puffy red cheeks that are filled with your salty eye rain.
I don't understand why you don't leave.
You have no bondage, nothing keeping you here.
You stay hidden away in the seller with no padlock.
You lay there screaming without a care.

But you don't want people to hear, you don't want
to leave.
As I bring you your meal you stare at me with those
water filled eyes.
You continue to scream as I put the food in your
mouth and move your mouth to eat.
As more food falls onto your shirt than in your
stomach I resent myself for letting you do this.
I leave and return, with a 12 gauge in my hand.
I ask you one more time if you want to leave, but
you stare at me with those wide eyes and open
mouth continuing to scream.
I pull the trigger and put you out of your misery.

Vulnerable

vul·ner·a·ble
/ˈvəlnər(ə)bəl/

1. Susceptible to physical or emotional attack or harm.
2. **Rocky Mullin** while writing this book.

Part 4

Reflection

re·flec·tion
/rəˈflekSH(ə)n/

1. The throwing back by a body or surface of light, heat, or sound without absorbing it.
2. Serious thought or consideration.

The silence within one's self is full of peace and bliss.
When one befriends their own soul the candle will never grow dim.
Inside of them they can find everything they searched for in the world.
The beauty of self is eternal.
Serenity in the company of your own skin.

THE MORNING AFTER.

I envision our nights ending swiftly while in each other's arms.

The weight of the day lies on us as we close our eyes and end asleep.

The day arrives with the light of the sun illuminating through our windows.

Shining stars into our eyes and the morning sun welcomes us to the new day.

The sound of sizzle and a boiling pot bring me out of my slumber and into your presence.

The smell of grease and coffee fill the air as my lungs are welcomed to the fresh beginning of another moon cycle.

I eagerly meet you as the life is sucked from me and flushes into you.

My life is yours.

FLEE.

God set me free years ago.

Allowing me to become the man I deemed worthy of being.

When that man fell short, he called me back, shaped me like clay, and created something only he and I knew.

The long nights of praying and tears brought me back and made me realize I am worthy of my dreams.

Worthy of passion, worthy of worth.

Through him, I am saved, through him I am Rocky.

He knew many years ago of the talks we'd have, the heartache I'd feel, and yet he still chose to listen and have conversations with me.

While my faith for him flows like a river, low and high.

He's had faith in me for lifetimes. Knowing he
would be the driving factor in what I am.
I pray for wisdom, and he made me wise.
Without him, I am just dirt in the ground.

VOW.

I am so alone I like to think that my future wife
prays that I meet no one before her.
That she gets on her knees at night and puts her
hands together.
Asks the lord to remove the placeholders from my
life until she can become the vision that lets my
eyes see.
That he guards me from those who will harm me
until she can make my life full.
So that my heart may attach to hers from miles
away and for that one moment late at night we are
one.
That our souls convene without meeting eye to eye.
That our future selves are smiling together.
The gift that is each other is paid back tenfold when
our lives combine into one.

I pray that she is praying for me, and that someday

we find our way home.

I LOVE YOU.

Hearing it from your mom is one thing, or your dad or grandma.

Even your aunts make it feel expected.

But hearing I love you from a stranger is a feeling like no other.

Someone that isn't inherently supposed to love you.

Someone you didn't know last year now loves you.

Human spirit and the soul create this love, not out of being forced, but by choice.

Someone loves you out of choice.

DELTA, BRAVO, CATHY, RINGO, SALLY.

I'm so thankful I can be a part of so many people's stories.

That my presence has altered their decisions.

My words have changed their thoughts.

That my shortcomings have helped them grow.

And as I look at old photographs, I feel like I'm looking at a puzzle that is full of the wrong pieces.

Because that puzzle no longer makes sense.

Those names don't go side by side.

Those hands don't interlock anymore.

Those people no longer exist.

I think about a kitten and its mother, does it
remember when it's old?
How its birth giver would nurse its strength so it
could survive on its own.
Does it remember how she would carry it around to
where it needed to be, guarding it from danger?
Does it miss the milk from its mother's body?
Does it have the memories that shaped it into the
animal it is today?
Has it forgotten the very thing that made it live?
When it goes to a new home does it reshape how it
was taught?
How can a cat bring life but forget it as well?
How can its purpose change the moment it's spawn
leaves the nest?
How can one animal create something, just to
forget it?

THE DEATH OF ROCKY MULLIN.

The thought of ending your life is something that
many feel, a thought many succeed at.
They chose to remove their soul from their body
with their own hands.
I chose to remove my body from my previous soul.
I chose to end my life and create a new one while
remaining on earth.
I walk the line that is death of oneself while still
breathing.
Creating something that is full of love, acceptance,
and Christ.
Removing greed and lust, regret and guilt.
Allowing the present to be what it will always be,
the present.
Giving my life new meaning and hopes.
Pushing the boundary of what is sane and insane.
Giving new ideas to the future me.

"While many can pursue their dreams in solitude, other dreams are like great storms blowing hundreds, even thousands of dreams apart in their wake. Dreams breathe life into men and can cage them in suffering. Men live and die by their dreams. But long after they have been abandoned they still smolder deep in men's hearts. Some see nothing more than life and death. They are dead, for they have no dreams."

Griffith.

Kentaro, Miura. *Berserk.* 1989.

Part 5

Reinvention

re·in·ven·tion
/ˌrēənˈvenSH(ə)n/

1. The action or process through which something is changed so much that it appears to be entirely new.

The Testimony of Rocky Mullin.

My great grandpa was a godly man. He read the bible more times than anyone I think I will ever meet. Knew where to find certain words, certain phrases, certain meanings. He had dozens of biblical books that pointed out everything in the Hebrew Bible, the King James Bible, the New International Version. Every single Bible. He read about the Muslims and the Jews and looked at their approach to religion. He never wavered, never frayed from his pursuit of God. When he died on New Year's day in 2022, I had zero fear of where he was. I knew that man was standing and walking with the Lord the moment his heart stopped beating. When I was younger, I would go over there, and he would preach to me. Tell me the stories of Moses and Joseph, about Job and Jonah.

The beginning and the end. I learned more from him than any Bible study group could ever teach me. Then the reign of ISIS in the middle east occurred. My great grandmother proceeded to tell an elementary school kid that someday a Muslim would take me, place me in shackles, and cut my head from my body if I didn't praise Allah. She made me swear in my heart that I would never denounce Jesus like Peter did. This petrified me, rightfully so. Since that day I have never forsaken Christ, I loved Christ, but I didn't understand the love of Christ. I loved Jesus because I was told that I would be beheaded, and I would rot in hell. The doomsday stories of Revelations and the End Times every weekend when I would go over there. So, one day I just decided to stop. I didn't go there anymore. In my teens I fell away from Christ, I still loved him, but I just didn't want to go to hell. My mother was never a church goer, she didn't like the idea of the Church. My other grandma loves God, she would have us in VBS and Sunday school every week. I went with flawless attendance, but I didn't go for my love of God, my friends went and there was free food. A very wise and amazing woman named Betty was my teacher at Mosby Baptist Church. She was patient and kind but could never show me the full love of God. So, I drifted, again. I still loved Christ, but I didn't LOVE Christ. When I was about 16 my life changed. I had sex for the first time, and this was a whole new world for me. I knew about saving yourself and the benefits of following God's path in marriage, but I didn't listen. Before I knew it, I had become hooked by the lust of beautiful women. If it was porn or Instagram models or women I knew. I loved the allure of a beautiful woman. I spilled my seed many times as the bible thumpers would say. This got me in lots and lots of trouble in my life. I felt so empty and alone. I would lay in bed next to a girl and feel like there wasn't anyone in a 50-mile vicinity of me. My heart urged for Christ, but I didn't know it yet. And eventually I got into a committed relationship, my first one, and eventually things led to us having sex. Sex is an integral part of any relationship, and I know this because I've experienced it. But at some point, it takes over and becomes a life of its own. You become new people during sex, you relinquish the people you were before to chase a climax of euphoria. The girlfriend I had eventually left me, she was right for it. I had nothing, no one. I didn't have a dime to pay for food and let alone someone to eat with. So, I read my bible. I turned away from being fearful of the contents and really READ the Bible. The same Bible that Ms. Betty couldn't get me to read years before. In the months after my big breakup, I found myself angry and betrayed. My friends had left me to pick the girl that left me. One night I was driving and was hysterically sad. I was all over the road and speeding and didn't really care what would happen next. One singular thought entered my head, "read the Bible." Now I was like 20-minutes away from home so that wasn't an option, but what was, was that my grandma's house was 5-minutes away. I got there and opened her Bible and flipped to a random page. After feeling extreme betrayal, anger, and bitterness. My finger landed on Psalm 54:5-7. The verses reads, "*He will repay my enemies for their evil. Cut them off in your truth. I will freely sacrifice to you; I will praise your name O Lord, for it is good. For he has delivered me out of all my trouble; and my eye has seen its desire upon my enemies.*" The overwhelming emotion that entered my body allowed me to do nothing but cry. Exactly what I needed to hear, in the exact moment I needed to hear it. This wouldn't be the first time I would learn that God's timing is exactly perfect. I swear to you this story is real. December 16th, 2020, at 6:37 P.M. I know this because I took a picture. This was the first real experience I had with God. You would think that this was the end of this story, and my life was turned around, and I became the perfect Christian, that is so far from the truth. This testimony is not a one and done thing. A walk with Christ leads you down many paths. Just as the Bible teaches us in many places like Romans, Colossians, or Exodus, a walk with Christ is lifelong. And my walk was just beginning.

The next few weeks I spent doing everything I could to learn about Christ. I watched the Passion of The Christ, I read some of the Gospels, I watched any video I could. But I couldn't seem to get that same connection I got in December. I chased it like a high. The holy spirit is a high like no other. I went to school, moved an entire state away, but wanted to continue to grow my roots in my faith. I read my bible there too, but eventually old wounds began to reopen. The pain and sadness I felt allowed me to indulge in a commonly used self-remedy, alcohol. I drank beer and seltzers and tequila and vodka. I would go to team meetings with a buzz, I would go to team dinner with a buzz, I would do anything to not feel the real emotions that were inside of me. I remember paying someone on my floor for vodka shots. I seriously gave him like $4 in ones just to get the sweet sweet taste of the cheapest thing a college kid could buy. Eventually, after alcohol poisoning and a 3-day hangover I had to stop. I confronted my losses and made a commitment to end this deadly journey I forced myself onto. I ended up leaving that school and football all together. You see, my life was decided by football. If I had practice that was my only focus. If I had a game? Don't even speak to me that day. Football was my life; football was my God. Leaving football was like abandoning the church for me. It was my savior and the only thing in my messed-up life that made me happy. I went home after that and really tried to work on myself but my anger and hate inside me overshadowed anything that was in my view. I still drank off and on and did those things; I was still sad. I started to get extremely into working out. I had worked out before but not like this. 3 times a day, 400mg of pre-work out 3 times a day, eat little amounts of food to lose weight. I lost a total of 45 lbs. in a 5-month span. This was before Ozempic or fad diets. I genuinely starved myself and forced my body to use the fat I had to fuel it. I was so insecure and lonely, I just wanted to be loved and the only way I knew how was to look good. On May 2nd, 2021 all of that finally came to fruition. I saw the girl that left me at my job and had a **MASSIVE** panic attack. I told people my heart had an irregularity from all the caffeine and terrible diet but the cats out of the bag, I had a panic attack. A bad one too, I went numb in all my limbs from hyperventilating, I couldn't see straight, my apple watch said my resting heart rate was like 164. Scary stuff. I went into the hospital after being picked up randomly from a buddy from High School. I was in the back of his truck praying to God that if this was it, allow me into his heavenly gates. Making a huge ask despite ignoring my faith for my worldly desires. The hospital suspected I was overdosing on cocaine or meth. I swiftly denied those claims, but they did a blood test anyway. Although my heart was fine, my kidneys were not. I was about 3% function away from dialysis, my doctor said. No more sugary drinks, no more creatine, no more sweet tea, no more Gatorade, no more pre workout. All gone, the tools that I used to shape the 184 lb. body I had spent months creating. Gone. After that I gained my weight back quickly. I was 200 lbs.

about 2 months later. That didn't change the fact that I had to change. Not only my diet but my life. I really thought I was about to die. So, from that day forward I chased Christ to catch back up in the walk we started earlier. Now, surely this is the end of the story, right? No. I had a LOT of catching up to do. So, as all good stories have, I met a girl. A beautiful woman. She loved God, she brought me to church, and we read the word together. There was just one issue, she was a sex addict. Genuinely. I know the dudes reading this are thinking that wow, this guy got to have sex everyday whenever he wanted? What is the issue? The issue was I literally felt my soul going further and further away from God every time. I felt my body cringe when she would make the beginning moves. I hated it. I hated myself for doing it. When we ended, I vowed to not have sex with a girl until we were at least dating for 3 months (Stupid).22 God by my side witnessing me trying to do better. God and I walked together after this, I truly felt the love of God. I was alone and I was okay with that. I knew that the man I wanted to be had to be molded and shaped by God. And then my life changed again. I couldn't go back to school. My one goal in life is to be the first person in my family to graduate college. Womp womp that's gone. So, I did what any 20-year-old kid does, and I went to work on the railroad. My friend had gotten me the job and it was fine, money was good. But I hated my life. I was alone and worked 12-hours a day to try and get back to the goal of graduating college. I made the money, had a solid 3k in my bank account and a letter in the mail came. A letter I am 100% certain was sent from God. My debt was forgiven. My chance at my dream had finally returned. I quit my job the next day and lived on that 3k that was for school. That summer, I met another girl. That girl was so kind and gentle and beautiful in every way. She was a Godly Oklahoman woman. But as all young people do, we ate the apple. But this felt different. I wasn't having sex out of pleasure; I was having sex because I cared for the person. That didn't make it right, I might have felt more fulfilled by this but deep, deep down I knew that my soul was hurting. I saw it was a slow stab every time that would eventually catch up to me. But as all good things do, it ended. She moved away, I couldn't get over my ex-girlfriend and we went our separate ways. I still couldn't shake the girl when I was 18 years old. She was an infection I couldn't get rid of. In December of 2022, 2 years after my journey began. We met again for the first time in 2 years. I'll save the boring details. We met, had coffee and went our separate ways. But I still wanted her. Desperately wanted her. After that I chased God again, hoping this time our walk would be everlasting. I prayed and I prayed. I loved God but I didn't LOVE God. I continued to learn and apply the Bible to my life, growing with poise and purpose. Until July of 2023. That month I returned to Psalm 54. I have never felt a wound like that before, a genuine stab in the back. Something I thought would never happen to me, I wasn't messy or sloppy. I might have had my issues but I kept it all pretty locked down, but this changed me. I prayed for my enemy's demise, I prayed their lives be taken from them, I prayed the lord abandon them. When in reality, the lord should have abandoned me. That month I slept with three different women, just to mask the pain and put on the idea that I was okay. I was convincing myself more than anyone else. On the last one, I felt empty and alone. Like my life had zero meaning. I was chasing my dream, an honor student in school, a caring young man. But all of that meant nothing because of the pain I felt after betrayal. I slept with that last girl, and I felt my soul leave. I was damned to hell; God had seen enough of me. But that was not true. I drove home crying, tears covered my shirt. I prayed to God to change me, to fix me, to make me whole. In Romans chapter 7 verse 15 it reads, "*I do not understand what I do. For what I want to do I do not do, but what I hate I do.*" I couldn't shake the fact that I sinned so much. Later in Romans chapter 8 it says in verse 18, "*or I consider that the sufferings of this present time are not worth comparing with the glory that is going to be revealed to us"*. The beauty in this is that regardless of my sin, I knew that good was going to come to mc. So that day, On July 20th, 2023, I promised to God I would not have sex for a year. Swore to it, told him if I lied to strike me down. On July 30th, 2024, I am proud to say I accomplished my promise to God. There were times that I wanted to and times I almost did, but in prayer I asked the lord to be my shepherd and to guide me and lead me away from temptation. Now you definitely think this story is over but it's not, I promise it's the last act. So, with that new promise under my belt and a head full of love for God I set out on my new journey, forgiveness. I held grudges like no other, I hated people. The man who betrayed me in July was first on my list to forgive. Jesus ate at the same table with Judas and knew he would betray him. So, I broke bread with my enemy. I hugged him and forgave him. I prayed for him to find God and let his path be shined upon. I had to forgive the girl who betrayed me, so I did. I didn't meet her until much later but by the time I did ,I had forgiven her. I pray for her happiness and love. That she finds her path in this messed up world. And by the time we did meet again, I was ready to break bread with her. I never understood the love of God or the fear of God. Why fear God if he loves me? Why love God endlessly if he'll always forgive me? In the span of 4-years everything was taken from me. Football, my girlfriend, my career chances, my education. God took those things away because he knew I wasn't ready. He knew that I wasn't the man I needed to be. He knew I didn't fear nor love him. He knew that I needed to be humbled and to learn life lessons. I used to pray for wisdom every single night, and God delivered. He showed me mercy and forgiveness, he showed me love and compassion. He taught me to fear that he can take everything and to love because he can give **ANYTHING**. I walk with zero fear now for I know the lord is right beside me in my walk with Christ. I know that with him my passions and goals are endlessly obtainable. With Christ by my side, I now understand the love of and FOR God.

The End of The Beginning.

About TwentyTwoTwos:

TwentyTwoTwos was created in August of 2023 to zero acknowledgement. No one knew what it was, what it would be, and who it was for. I created this as an outlet for myself to create things that no one would expect. With titles like, "*The End of Us, Was The Beginning of Me*" or "*Depar*", I used my small platform to write things I felt passionate about. While TTT is still technically an independent small entertainment company, it is far more than just that. TwentyTwoTwos is a brand run by Rocky Mullin. It is something that I created as a passion project that turned into my life's goal. In April of 2024 I spoke to a close friend of mine, Chris Paige, about my dream for the brand. For it to become a place artists, and filmmakers, and authors, and anyone really can come to grow, build, and promote their works. With the goal of giving somebody a place to let their art live. I knew this would be no small feat and I would first have to build my own brand and image first. The release of my first book was met with zero response other than people I knew or random people who clicked the link in my Instagram; But that gave me so much more. It was a liftoff point that shaped the TTT we know today. The brand that within the end of the year will have its first real book release, a podcast, a short film, and photography (Barring anything setting back production). With the help of my creative consultant, Jordyn Navarro, I plan to build the brand to become something that not only I can be proud of but others as well. The goal is to inspire others to create. Although this process is extremely long and thorough, I have full confidence that not only will the viewers of all the content love it, but will feel inspired to do something of their own. I thank you for taking the time to read my book and further the development of TwentyTwoTwos, your contribution will forever leave a mark of thanks on my soul. Until the next one.

-Rocky Mullin.

Owner of TwentyTwoTwos

Follow us on our social media platforms.

Instagram:

@Rocky.Mullin

@Jordynnavarro

@TwentyTwoTwos_

TikTok:

@Rocky.Mullin

@TwentyTwoTwosPub

YouTube:

@TwentyTwoTwosPub

Published by TwentyTwoTwos Publishing

TwentyTwoTwos is a publishing brand out of Kansas City, MO

This is the 10th iteration of this book.

This first publishing of this book is September 15th, 2024

TwentyTwoTwos Publishing

Published in the United States of America

Although It Rains, I Still Want to Dance
2025.

9 798227 053534

Printed by Libri Plureos GmbH in Hamburg,
Germany